To Precious Girls everywhere—
may your hearts remain honest and
pure so that your actions and
words reflect who you are.

Nothing But the Truth

By Cindy Kenney

Illustrated by the Precious Moments Creative Studio

Library of Congress Control Number: 2009925291

Kenney, Cindy, *Nothing But the Truth* / Cindy Kenney for Precious Moments, Inc.
Precious Moments # 990048 (Tradepaper)
          # 990047 (Hardcover)

ISBN 978-0-9817159-8-8 (Tradepaper)
ISBN 978-0-9817159-9-5 (Hardcover)

Printed in China

Table of Contents

CHAPTER ONE

Truth or Dare

"Wow, Kirina!" I said, joining my friends in a round of applause as she did several cartwheels across my front lawn.

Kirina stood up, took a bow, and joined in the laughter as she completed her dare.

We were playing *Truth or Dare* as we waited for my dad to come home and let us in. Every Friday after school, the Precious Girls Club got together for our weekly meeting. My mom and Aunt Ella helped me start the group when we moved to Shine, Wisconsin, last summer.

"Okay, it's your turn, Katie!" Kirina smiled. "Truth or dare?"

I gulped and wondered what she might ask or dare me, then answered, "Truth."

"Make it a good one, Kirina!" Bailey and Nicola called out as everyone huddled around to listen.

"What's your most embarrassing moment?" Kirina asked.

I looked at the good friends I'd made since the Precious Girls Club began at the start of the school season. We sure had been through a lot! Then I remembered my most embarrassing moment.

"It was shortly after I moved here," I began. "I was trying to start this group—the Precious Girls Club. I worked super hard on the flyers, posters, and the first meeting—but no one came. I was way embarrassed. I'm still surprised my mom and Aunt Ella convinced me to give it another try!"

"Oh, Katie, that makes me feel just awful!" Nicola said, reaching over to give me a little hug.

"Me too!" came the same answer from others.

"Gee, that's more embarrassing for us than it is for you!" Kirina said.

"I'm glad you worked so hard on getting to know each of us so that we all came to your next meeting," Bailey said.

"When is your dad going to get here?" Jenny asked, changing the subject.

"I don't know. He knows we're meeting after school. He promised my mom and Aunt Ella that he'd be here to let us in before Mom left to go out of town," I answered.

"Well, I'm very thirsty. How long are we supposed to wait?" Jenny asked.

I suddenly felt embarrassed again. I was relieved to finally see my dad's car turn the corner and head toward us.

"Here he is!" I announced.

"Sorry I'm late, girls," my dad said as he hurried over with several grocery bags.

"What happened, Dad? We've been here for nearly an hour waiting for you."

He looked at my friends who wondered the same thing.

"Well, ummm . . . I tried to get out of work, but someone needed my help and kept me late. I'm really sorry. Am I forgiven?"

"Yes," I said, grabbing a bag as I put my arm around his waist.

We all headed inside and dug into the treats he had bought at the store.

"So what have you girls been doing to keep busy?"

"We were playing *Truth or Dare*, Mr. Bennett," Becca answered. "Want to play?"

"Gee, I'm not sure. How do you play?" Dad answered.

"You choose whether we give you a question you have to answer truthfully, or a dare you have to do," Avery answered.

"That sounds easy enough," my dad answered, clueless about what he was getting himself into. "I guess I'll pick *truth*. That sounds a lot safer than a dare."

The girls laughed. Maybe he understood the game better than I thought. We huddled together to come up with a question.

"Okay, Dad. What are you most afraid of?"

He thought for a minute and answered. "I'm probably afraid of more things than you realize, but I'd have to say my biggest fear is losing my family due to some sort of accident or disaster."

"Awwwww," came a chorus of female voices as I gave my dad a little squeeze.

"Now it's your turn to give a truth or a dare to someone, Mr. Bennett," Lidia explained.

"Okay, I've got one for everyone."

"That's not how you play, Dad," I said.

"Hear me out, kiddo. Instead of giving all of you a dare, I've got more of a challenge."

"What is it?"

"What do you mean?"

"Tell us!"

My dad reached into his pocket and pulled out a piece of paper. "I received this invitation at Camp SonShine. I thought it might be of interest to the Precious Girls Club."

The reason we had moved to Shine was so my dad could take a new job as the director of Camp

SonShine on Lake Lightning. It is a pretty cool job that lets him spend more time with us.

"This is an invitation from the President of the United States," he began. "It's for kids' groups all across the nation."

"The President of the United States?" Jenny asked.

"That's right. Here, I'll read part of the letter.

The President is looking for several children's groups that exemplify what it means to be model citizens in today's community.

In an effort to encourage students to use their talents and skills to the best of their ability, the President will be looking for groups that demonstrate honor, integrity, and service to others.

The President will select ten model groups to represent Today's Students for a Better Tomorrow. Winners will be included in a promotional brochure and DVD, and will receive an official visit from the President of the United States who will visit their school to speak and present them with an award.

Interested groups must submit an official appli-cation and a five-minute DVD illustrating why their group should be chosen . . .

"There's a bit more about the application process. So, are you interested?"

"Would we really have a chance?"

"Well sure, why not?"

"Of course we do," Jenny interrupted. "Why wouldn't we?"

Jenny McBride liked to think she could do any-thing and everything better than everyone else, just because her dad owns several big businesses in downtown Shine.

"I think it's worth trying. You have just as much chance as anyone else. You've done a lot of good things since you started the Precious Girls Club."

"How can we make a five-minute DVD, Mr. Bennett?" Bailey asked.

"I've got some equipment at the camp that we

can use, but it would be up to you girls to decide what to include in it."

"Let's show a few seconds of our individual talents and then the rest of the time show what we've done as a group," I said.

"Great! Next week at Camp SonShine we start working on the float for the Independence Day parade. I'll get some good footage of you working on that."

"What a cool idea!" Lidia said. "And it's very patriotic."

Everyone started talking at once. The idea was a big hit.

"The entire group will be evaluated in addition to each member who must submit an application," my dad explained. "You must each answer questions and include a few paragraphs about why you think the Precious Girls Club should be chosen."

"Oh no," Becca said.

"What's wrong?"

"My grades aren't very good this year," she admitted.

"And I'm lousy at math," I added.

"Oh great," Jenny moaned.

I could feel my cheeks get hot as everyone turned to look at me.

"Whoa! Hold on!" Dad said. "This isn't about getting good grades. There's a place to include your grades, but they're much more interested in the things you've accomplished."

I could tell Becca wasn't convinced. I was still a little worried too.

"Girls, this is about what you do with the gifts God has given you—which is what the Precious Girls Club is all about—using your individual talents to do good in the world around you. Right?"

Nicola was reading the application and said, "Your dad is right, Katie. The application is about what we have accomplished individually and as a group, along with our essay about why we think we should win."

"Essay? I thought it was just a couple of paragraphs?" Kirina said. "I'm a horrible writer!"

"Avery can help us," I said, offering her

assistance. "She won this year's writing contest!"

"Would you, Avery?" Kirina asked.

"Sure, if you want me to," Avery said.

"You can all help each other," my dad said. "That's all part of working as an effective group."

Everybody pitched in to clean up and headed outside to wait for rides home.

"We have to list all of our awards and accomplishments on this application," Jenny said, reading hers. "Why don't we bring whatever awards we've won to our next meeting? We can display them and your dad can film them!"

"Great idea, Jenny!" Kirina said. "I'll bring my gymnastics and soccer awards!"

"Avery, you can bring your new writing award!" I said.

"I'm not sure if we should focus just on trophies and awards," Nicola said.

"What do you mean?" Jenny asked. "That's what this contest is all about."

"No, that's only part of it. It's about doing the

best we can with the talents we've got. It's about being good citizens and building a good future for ourselves and others. That's something we can do without ever winning an award."

"You're right," I agreed.

Jenny made a face. "What's wrong, Nicola? Don't you have an award you can bring to show the group?"

Nicola scowled at her. "Yes, I've got awards I can bring. That's *not* the point."

"I have an idea," I said, trying to keep the peace. "Let's bring things that best represent who we are. If that includes an award, that's fine—but it doesn't have to."

"What do you mean?" Lidia asked.

"Well, Avery can bring the story she wrote plus the award she won for it."

"Okay, but that still revolves around an award," Becca noted.

"Lidia can bring the science project she had on display at the fair. Bailey can bring the big family cookbook she made for everyone at Christmas. Nicola can bring the pretty scarf she learned to knit. Oh, and we can all wear our Precious Girls bracelets that show what we've done!"

"Those are hobbies," Jenny protested.

"Some are," Nicola said. "But they also show who we are and what we do with our talents!"

The girls agreed. Well, most of them did. Jenny still wanted to center everything on trophies and awards, and everyone was excited about that.

I noticed Bailey sitting on the porch, looking a little sad, so I headed over and sat beside her on the swing. "How come you're so quiet? Is something wrong?"

"No, I'm fine," she said, holding my kitten, Sparky, and choking back a tear.

"What's wrong? Are you okay?"

She shook her head and turned away from me. I couldn't figure out what had happened to make her cry.

"Bailey! Talk to me. I can't help if you don't tell

me what's wrong."

"I'm just not in a good mood. I had a bad day in school, and now I'm taking it out on you," she said. "I'm sorry, I didn't mean to act so dumb."

"It's not dumb," I assured her as a car pulled up in front of the house.

"That's my mom," she said. "Thanks for everything."

"Are you sure you're okay?" I called.

"I'll be fine!" she said, heading toward the car. "It's the weekend, right?"

"Absolutely!" I agreed and waved good-bye.

Yes, it absolutely is the weekend, but something is also absolutely wrong. The question is what?

CHAPTER TWO

Bailey's Dilemma

My dog, Patches, and I headed up to my bedroom to get my chores done so I could enjoy the rest of the weekend. I knew my mom would come home from her trip and freak out if she saw it so messy.

I leaned over to pick up dirty clothes and saw a flash of color whoosh by and a splash of twinkling swirl around me.

"Faith!"

"Yes, that's me!" she said, zipping this way and that, trying to make me laugh.

"You're cleaning your room before your mom gets home, right?" she asked.

"May as well. It will save me the lecture, plus I'd have to do it then anyway," I groaned.

"Well, I'm glad," Faith said. "Otherwise, one of these days you won't be able to find me in here!"

"That will never happen," I assured her.

Faith is my guardian angel and best friend. She was a gift to me from my dad when we moved to Shine. Trying to cheer us up, he gave my sister, Anna, and me the most beautiful angels that danced about in a musical snow globe.

One day when I was feeling especially sad about moving, Faith sprang to life right in front of me! It was amazing!

I know it's hard to believe, but it really happened. The hardest part is that no one else can see or hear Faith—except for me.

"Hey, Munchkin! I heard your Precious Girls Club is applying for a visit from the President of the United States!" Faith said.

Faith is so helpful, kind, and sweet. I don't know what I would do without her.

"Yes, we're going to apply. We'll see what happens.

"Did you see Bailey when she went home?" she asked me.

"Yes. She looked really exaserbated."

"I think you mean exasperated," Faith laughed.

"Ooops! Yeah, that's the word! Do you think I said something to upset her?"

"Beats me. Why don't you ask her? You like to talk when there's something bothering you," Faith said.

"You're right, I do. I'll finish up my chores and go over to her house."

"Sounds good to me," Faith winked.

So I cleaned my room, took out the garbage, watered my mom's plants, and dusted the furniture. Then I asked Dad if I could visit Bailey. He said yes and I left.

• • •

"Hi, Katie! What's up?" Bailey asked.

"Why don't you tell me?"

"What do you mean?" she asked.

There was an uncomfortable silence.

"C'mon, Bailey, don't pretend," I said. "It was obvious something was bothering you when you left today."

It took some encouraging, but finally Bailey opened up to me. I was surprised to hear her say that she felt she wasn't good at anything or special in any way.

Bailey was the youngest of six brothers and sisters. Her older siblings got better grades and won awards for everything—sports, music, Scouts, and dance. Bailey didn't feel like she fit in. I remembered how much convincing it took to get her to come to the Precious Girls Club.

Bailey was not only shy, but she thought no one wanted her in the club. It took a lot of reassuring her that we did.

"Bailey, can I ask you something?"

"Sure, go ahead."

"Do you believe that God made everyone special and unique?"

Bailey thought for a minute. "Unique, yes."

"Not special?"

"I don't know. I guess it depends on how you define it."

"I wish you could see yourself through the eyes of others, Bailey."

Another uncomfortable moment, then Bailey laughed. "I don't like to look at myself—period."

"Bailey, cut it out!" I said.

"Why? It's who I am, Katie. My whole family

thinks I'm a disaster."

"They do not."

"Yes, they do. Except for my mom, but she has to love me. Those are the mom rules or something."

"I like who you are. Are you saying that I have bad taste in friends?"

"You said it, not me."

I was so frustrated with her! She was acting way stubborn. It made no sense, but then, I didn't know what it was like to be the youngest of a big family either. Maybe it was harder than I thought.

"Bailey, you're a good friend to me. That's special about you. Look at all you've done in our club. You came up with funny jokes when we did the puppet show for the kids at the hospital. You made tons of beautiful gifts for the residents of the nursing home. You sing way better than I do. I found that out when we went Christmas caroling."

"But I've never won a single award or trophy."

"Who cares?"

"I do, Katie. Everyone else is going to bring

their awards to the meeting next week. Everyone but me."

"We're bringing more than just that, remember? You can bring stuff from your farm. You know how to do stuff around here that none of us know how to do."

I stayed for pizza when her parents invited me to join them for dinner. I think Bailey was glad I stayed, but I could tell I hadn't done much to convince her that she was just as special as everyone else.

I told her that God made everyone special, but then she said that she was letting God down. It was obvious that I couldn't change her mind.

I left, feeling bad that I had not been successful. Did that make *me* a bad friend?

I really did not know.

CHAPTER THREE

Caught in a Lie

"Hi, honey. Welcome home!" I heard my dad say when I woke late Saturday morning.

My mom had returned from her trip to the old neighborhood.

"How was your trip?"

"Terrific, but I missed you. Everything okay?"

"Of course. Here, let me help you with that."

I was anxious to hear about my mom's trip, so I slipped into my fuzzy slippers, put on my robe, and headed downstairs.

"You were that late? Chuck, I told you the girls would be coming over right from school," my mom said.

"I realize that," my dad answered. "I just lost track of the time. When Al called to ask me to go golfing, I never thought we'd be out on the course that long."

"Out on the course?" I said, coming into the kitchen. "You were golfing? Dad, you told us you couldn't get away from work."

There was an awkward pause as my mom glared at my dad and he sat there, looking very guilty.

"Shame on you, Dad," Anna teased, as she flipped something on the stove.

I could not believe I had just caught my dad in a lie! I wasn't sure how to handle it.

"Guilty as charged," he said at last. "I shouldn't have lied, Pumpkin. I guess I felt bad for being late and didn't want you and the girls to think I'd forgotten about you."

"But that's what you did," I frowned.

"Yes, I did," he confessed again. "And it was wrong of me. I'll come clean to the whole group on Friday."

"Really?" I asked surprised.

"Really," he promised.

"Well, it's over now. I don't think you have to

say anything at this point, Dad."

"Yes, I do. I'm not a very good example if I don't come clean when I've done something wrong. I'd rather apologize and let everyone know I'm sorry for what I did."

"Okay," I agreed. "Thanks Dad."

He came over and gave me a big hug.

"Hey, what about me?" Mom asked, pulling Anna over to join me and Dad for a big group hug.

Mom told me all about her trip as Anna served us breakfast. I ate French toast until my stomach

felt like it would burst. It was nice sharing breakfast together.

• • •

Back in my room, I asked Faith why she thought
Bailey felt so bad when I told her she was just as
special as everyone else.

"There are many things that make people feel
that way, Munchkin. I'm just glad you were a good
friend to her."

"But I don't think I helped at all."

"Sure you did. You were a good listener.
Everybody needs that."

"But I don't think I made her feel any better,
Faith."

"You might be surprised. Just having someone
there to listen and offer friendship means a lot."

"I hope so. Faith, if God makes everyone special in some way, why do some people still make
bad decisions or choose to do things wrong?"

Faith did several flips in the air as she made her
way over to me. Then she asked, "Have you ever

done something wrong?"

I rolled my eyes and said, "You know I have."

"Have you ever been crabby?" she asked.

"Yes, you know that too."

"Have you ever chosen to watch television, instead of cleaning your room like your mom asked you to do?"

"Of course! What's your point?"

"Have you ever been jealous of your sister or not shared something with her?"

"Faith! You're asking questions that you know the answers to."

"Okay, just one more," Faith smiled. "Why did you do those things?"

I thought for a minute. That answer was harder than the others. I didn't know.

"Beats me. To get my way, I guess. I'm not perfect."

"That's right. God made everyone special—not perfect. He loves us so much that He lets us make our own choices. God hopes that we will love Him enough to make good choices."

I thought about it. I knew God loved us a lot and gave us so much. Still it did not make sense why some people did such terrible things.

Faith pointed out that temptation plays a big role. It makes everything confusing and tries to get us to do wrong.

"So how do we stay on the right path, Faith?"

"Ah! That's why it's important to stay close to God. You can do that by talking to Him, especially when you feel tempted to do something wrong. Prayer is a wonderful thing!"

"I always feel better when I pray," I told Faith. "It makes me feel closer to God."

"Exactly. And you can go to church, read your Bible, or talk to other people who trust God."

"That makes sense. Thanks, Faith."

"You are welcome!" she said zooming across the room. "Keep being a friend to Bailey. That's important too. It's important to show others small acts of kindness."

Suddenly, my doorknob jiggled and I heard a loud knock.

"Mom?"

"No, it's me, Anna. Let me in, will you?"

I opened the door. Anna and a girl stood there. The girl was holding Anna's angel snow globe.

"That's my sister, Katie. Katie, this is my friend Kara."

We both said hello.

"Where's your angel snow globe? I want to show Kara. She's really into snow globes and she loves the one Dad got me."

I walked over to my shelf and picked up Faith who winked at me from inside the globe.

"Oooo, she's pretty!" Kara admired.

"The music is different in both of them," Anna explained. "And each angel looks much different."

"But they're both so beautiful."

"Which one do you like best?" I asked.

Kara examined the two angels. "It's hard to say. They both look so pretty."

"I think mine is prettier," I said. "She's really special too."

I really wanted to tell them just how special, but Faith said I couldn't. If I told others about Faith, no one would believe me.

Kara smiled and said they were both wonderful. Then she and Anna left.

After they were gone, I heard Faith say, "No contest."

"What?" I asked, turning around.

"No contest," Faith repeated. "I'm much prettier."

It made me giggle to hear Faith talk that way. "You're both gorgeous," I told her. "I'm glad it's not a contest."

I opened a book and started to read, but I could still hear Faith mumbling about something. I think she said, "Not a contest? We'll see about that!"

CHAPTER FOUR

Floating on a Lie

My dad was waiting for the Precious Girls Club when we gathered for our next meeting. He started out by confessing the lie he told last week and apologized to everyone. They all forgave him.

He showed us the flatbed in the barn where we would build the float for the 4th of July parade. Aunt Ella arrived with craft materials and tons of tissue paper. She taught us how to make tissue paper flowers as we brainstormed ideas for the float.

We decided to make a float that would show how everybody in the whole world was special. It was a cool idea and we were excited about it.

As we went to work on the float, the girls started to talk about my dad's confession and apology.

"Your dad is pretty cool to confess like that, Katie," Becca said.

"Yes, my dad would never admit that he lied to

someone," Kirina laughed.

"It wasn't even a bad lie," Nicola added.

"The reason he confessed was because he feels honesty is important," I told my friends.

"Some lies are good," Jenny said. "If someone asks if they look nice, but they don't, you don't say they look terrible."

"In that case it would be hurtful to tell the truth," Lidia said.

"But if we should always be honest, what about those situations?" Jenny asked.

I just shrugged. I really didn't know.

"I've got a good one," Kirina said. "When we go out to eat with someone, my dad always says, 'If you can get the check, I'll pick up the next one.'"

Everybody laughed.

"How about when someone says, 'How are you?'" Becca said. "It's not like they really want to hear how you are."

"Or when someone says they'll call you later, but they never do," I added.

We all agreed that people tell a lot more little lies than they realize.

"Even commercials lie," Bailey said. "This is the best product you'll ever use!"

"My little brother is always the first to say, 'I didn't do it' when he's usually the one who did!" Lidia laughed.

"When my dad goes fishing, he always says that the fish he caught were *this big!* But when my mom cleans them, we never see any that are even close to that size," Jenny laughed.

"My mom lies about her age," Nicola said. "She hates for anyone to know how old she is."

Aunt Ella asked if we were ready for a break. The time had gone by quickly.

"While you eat your brownies, why don't you share the things you brought to show the group about how each one of you is special?" she said.

We grabbed what we brought, got a treat, and sat in a circle. My dad prepared to film us as we each had our moment to talk about ourselves. It was fun to see and hear about the items that everyone brought. We had a very talented group! There were many awards, but there were other cool things that showed even more about the person who brought them.

Some of the girls were good at sports, others were great dancers, cooks, helpers, singers, actresses, seamstresses, crafters, swimmers, musicians, and even comedians. The list went on and on.

After I finished sharing the things I brought, it was Bailey's turn.

"Come on, Bailey, it's your turn," Nicola encouraged. "What did you bring?"

Bailey reached into the bag and pulled out a huge trophy!

I had to do a double-take. This wasn't just any trophy—it was enormous! I'm not sure I had ever seen one that big.

"Wow!" everyone gasped.

"I won this last year when we were on vacation," she explained. "My whole family entered a

big race, but I won the kid's division."

"My gosh, Bailey, I didn't know you could run that fast!" Kirina said.

"I trained a lot last year because my entire family entered the race," Bailey said quietly.

It felt like she was trying to avoid looking at me, and with good reason. I knew she said she had never won anything in her life, but if that was the case, where did the huge trophy come from?

I leaned closer to read what it said, but it just said *First Place.* I couldn't wait to talk to her about it some more.

Although Bailey was very shy and humble about her trophy at first, she opened up more and more as the group gathered around her with their "Oooo's" and "Ahhhh's." By the time she finished talking about it, she made herself sound like Rocky Balboa training for the big fight. I could almost hear the theme music in the background as she spoke.

"Nice job!" my dad said, turning off the camera.

"Time to clean up. Turn your applications in to me. Mrs. Bennett will read over your essays and answers to make sure everything is complete. I'm proud of all of you. What a group!"

"Thanks, Mr. Bennett!" Bailey said, still glowing from all the praise.

While everyone pitched in to clean up, I made several attempts to pull Bailey aside and ask her what was up, but she was very good at avoiding me. She was the first to leave.

Why would Bailey make up a story like that? Was there a chance she had forgotten she had won the award? That was impossible. I sure did want to find out what was up with that trophy.

CHAPTER FIVE

Who's the Best?

My bedroom was decorated with lovely streamers and butterflies hanging from the ceiling. Beautifully colored flower bunches were sitting everywhere.

"What's going on?" I said.

Faith zipped from one end of the room to the other, did a triple flip, and landed on the bed. "Ta da!" she said. "You like it?"

"You did all this?"

"Of course. I had to," she answered.

"But why?"

"For the big contest," Faith explained.

"What contest?"

"The angel contest! When the judges come to see where I am living, I want it to be impressive," she explained.

"What judges? Faith, what contest?"

"You started it," she said.

"Me?" I asked.

"Yes! Don't you remember? Your sister and her friend stopped by and you asked which one was the best!"

"But I didn't mean . . ."

"Didn't mean what? You're not going to lose confidence in me now are you?" Faith said, looking a little hurt.

"No! It's just that I had no idea . . ."

"I've been working all day on my dance routine," Faith interrupted. "Wait until you see what I'm wearing for the swimsuit competition!"

"You're having a swimsuit competition?"

"Of course, silly," Faith giggled. "I'm dancing for the talent show. This is my evening gown for the show."

I didn't understand, but I needed to talk to Faith about Bailey. I told her everything.

"What bothers you the most about what Bailey did?" Faith asked.

"I think she lied! How could she have forgotten about winning that award?"

"It does sound unlikely," Faith agreed.

"She was glowing when everyone gathered to see the trophy and listen to her story. She looked so happy. I don't want to ruin that."

"Then don't," Faith said, distracted.

"What do you mean?"

"Just treat her honestly and see what she says in return."

"You make it sound simple."

"Isn't it?"

"I don't think so," I mumbled.

"Let me know how it turns out," Faith said. "I have to rehearse my dance."

Faith zipped this way, that way, and then in a cloud of sparkling dust, she disappeared back into the snow globe.

I was so confused!

"Katie," my dad called. "It's time to go!"

My dad was taking us out to a drive-in movie. I was glad to have something fun to take my mind off all of this.

I reached for my pink sweater and headed out the door, but turned to look at all the pretty decorations again.

Hmmm, I thought. *An angel contest?*

CHAPTER SIX

Little Fib or a Big Fat Lie?

It was the last week of school before summer vacation. Everyone was excited. Kids were sharing stories about where they were going or what their plans were for the summer, but there was something else going on too.

Word was out about Bailey's super-big trophy. She loved every minute of it.

As I twirled the jump rope, I watched small groups of kids run up to Bailey to get her story about how she won her award.

When the bell rang, I headed over to her, but I was too late. She had just launched into another retelling of the big race. As I listened, I was certain some of the details of the race had changed. The course suddenly had big hills she had to run up, and it was now a 10k instead of just a 5k.

"Slow down," I called to Bailey at lunchtime.

"You can't escape talking to me forever."

Bailey sat down to eat her lunch. "I don't know what you mean. I'm not avoiding you, Katie."

"Right," I huffed. "Where have you been? I've been calling you since Friday."

"I've been busy on school stuff. I have two final projects to turn in," she said.

"Every time I called, your brothers and sisters said you were out."

"They never know where anyone is, Katie. You can't believe a thing they say."

"I'm glad you brought that up," I said.

"Brought what up?"

"Believing what people say. I believed you last week when you said you'd never won an award. I felt terrible for you. What's up with that Bailey? Were you lying to me then, or were you lying to the girls in the Precious Girls Club?"

"Neither, Katie. It's just one little award that I'd forgotten about because I won it while we were on vacation."

"Bailey, the word "little" does not describe that trophy. How could you possibly forget something that big?"

"Are you accusing me of lying? I thought you were my friend, Katie."

"I am your friend. That's why I want you to tell me the truth. I don't care whether you won a dumb old trophy or not," I tried to get her to tell me the truth.

"It's not a dumb trophy, Katie. Just ask anybody."

"I'm asking you, Bailey. Friends are straight with each other."

"Okay, then believe me because I forgot I won it. I was having a lousy day last week and just forgot."

"Forgot about what?" Jenny McBride asked, as she joined us for lunch.

That was the end of our privacy. I knew I could push it, but I kept my mouth shut. Bailey is my friend. I wasn't going to embarrass her.

Later in gym class, a girl named Kathleen ran up to Bailey. Kathleen was a star on the girl's track team. "I want to introduce you to the track coach. I heard about the huge trophy you won last summer. We can use another good runner on the team!"

"I don't really have time for that," Bailey said shyly.

Kathleen disappeared, but returned with Mrs. Drake, the track coach. She introduced her to Bailey, hoping that maybe she'd convince Bailey to participate.

"How about if you join us after school today and run the track a few times with Kathleen?" Mrs. Drake asked. "Let me just get some times on you, and then we can discuss the possibilities."

"Umm . . . I've got chores on my farm," Bailey said. "I really don't think I can."

"Well, talk to your folks, and see if tomorrow works, okay?" Mrs. Drake asked.

"Sure, I'll see."

I wondered what would happen to Bailey if everyone found out she had lied. At this point, it was a lot more than a little fib. It had turned into a big fat lie.

CHAPTER SEVEN

Super Sleuth

When I got home, I tried to talk to Faith about Bailey, but she was so wrapped up in her own contest that she was only half-listening.

"What's going on, Faith?" I said at last.

"What do you mean?"

"I don't understand why you're so into this contest," I said.

"I'm just following your lead, Munchkin."

"What do you mean?"

"You showed me how important it is to win stuff—you know, be the best!"

"No, I didn't."

"Sure you did. When Anna brought her friend over, the first thing you asked was which angel she liked better."

"So?"

"And you pointed out that I was the prettiest!"

she smiled.

"You are!"

"Exactly! I should prove it too."

"Whatever. Will you come with me to talk with Bailey? I could use your support."

"I have a lot to do."

"Please, Faith? Mom asked me to return a pan to Bailey's mom, so it's the perfect time to talk to her again."

"I suppose, if we won't be long."

"Deal."

• • •

When I got to Bailey's farm, no one answered when I knocked. I headed around back to see if anyone was there. Mrs. Walters was hanging laundry on the clothesline.

"Katie! What a delight to see you, dear."

I pulled her pan out of my backpack, and said, "Nice to see you, too, Mrs. Walters. My mom asked that I return this to you."

"Oh, thank you so much for bringing it over."

"Is Bailey home?"

"Oh, I'm sorry, honey. Her dad just took her to a dentist appointment. I'll tell her you dropped by."

"Okay, thanks!"

I headed back to my bike with Faith who flitted about beside me. A car was just pulling into the driveway. It was Bailey's older sister.

"Hi, Hannah!"

"Hi, Katie, Bailey's not here."

"Your mom just told me," I said. Then an idea hit me. "Hey Hannah, do you know where Bailey keeps that big trophy she won?"

Hannah turned and frowned. "I'm sorry, Katie, but I don't know what you're talking about."

"Last week Bailey brought a huge trophy to show us at the Precious Girls Club. It was really something!"

"Bailey never won any trophy. You must be thinking of someone else."

I knew it! I just knew that Bailey had lied. Despite my discovery, I didn't want to embarrass her.

"Oh, that's right. She said one of her sisters had won it."

"Oh, you probably mean my trophy then! About this big?" she said showing the size with her hands.

"That's the one. Congratulations!"

"Thanks, it's just one of a bunch of them, though."

"That's what she said."

"Why do you want to see it again?"

"I just thought it was cool. I never saw a trophy that big before."

"She had no right to take it without asking," Hannah was irritated.

"She was so proud of you, Hannah. Please don't tell her I told you," I begged.

"Well, okay," she agreed. "This time only. It's nice to hear she feels that way."

"She went on and on about how great you are," I said, realizing that now I was lying too!

But it did the trick. Hannah was very pleased

to hear this, and I hoped she wouldn't spill the beans.

On the way home, I felt a sharp twinge on my ear as Faith gave me a little flick of her finger.

"What was that for?"

"Why are *you* lying now?" Faith asked.

"It didn't hurt anyone, Faith. It was just a little lie."

"Really? I don't recall God saying, 'Don't ever lie—unless it's just a little thing that doesn't matter too much.'"

"I know, I'm sorry. I didn't even realize what I was doing until it was too late. I won't do it again, honest."

I really meant it. But at the moment, the bigger issue was what to do with the truth now that I had it!

CHAPTER EIGHT

Limping Along

School let out and everyone was anxious for fun! The Precious Girls Club decided to get together for a picnic at the beach on Lake Lightning.

We were all excited about showing off our new swimsuits and seeing who would be hanging out on the beach this year. It was a perfect day that felt like nothing could ruin it. We flew kites and tossed around a Frisbee. The water was cool, the sun was hot, and even our soggy sandwiches tasted great.

We decided to play *Truth or Dare* again while we ate. It was our group's favorite new game.

Somebody dared Becca to run to the water and dive in without stopping. Kirina had to tell the truth about what boy she most hoped to see at the beach. Becca had to crab walk to the lifeguard station and back again. Jenny told the truth about how much her swimsuit actually cost.

Jenny chose Bailey next. "Truth or dare?"

"Truth," Bailey said.

Jenny gazed at her with a challenging look and said, "Tell us the truth. What's the biggest lie you've ever told?"

Bailey and I gave Jenny a sharp look, worried that she knew something.

"That's a weird question, Jenny," Nicola said, munching on potato chips.

"Yes, besides, who could possibly judge that?" Lidia asked.

"Just answer the question," Jenny said.

"I'm thinking," Bailey mumbled as she glanced in my direction.

I had no idea how to help her. As it turned out, I didn't have to.

"Hey, trophy girl!" someone shouted.

We all looked up and saw Kathleen and a big bunch of kids heading our way.

"Do you guys want to play freeze tag?"

Relieved that she didn't have to answer Jenny's

question, Bailey immediately said, "Sure! I mean, what do you guys think?"

We were all willing and knew it was a great way to get heated up before jumping in the water.

Kathleen helped Bailey up and said, "You're on

my team! Come on."

The game began, but it quickly became obvious that Bailey didn't look like a track star and was struggling to keep up with most of us.

"Time out!" Kathleen called. She headed over to Bailey, who stood frozen, waiting to be tagged so she could play again.

"What's wrong with you?" she asked. "You're hardly moving."

Bailey looked around as everyone started walking toward her.

"I sprained my ankle this morning. I thought it was better, but it's not," she lied again. "I'm really sorry. I thought I could play, but I guess not."

"You better ice that, girl!" Kathleen told her. "You have to take care of yourself."

Kathleen helped her over to a bench while the rest of us finished the game. When we were done, Kathleen reminded Bailey to get rest and waved good-bye, as we all jumped into the water.

Afterward, we decided there was no better way

to end the day than to top it off at the ice cream parlor. I offered to hang back with Bailey who needed more time to get there.

The closer we got to the ice cream parlor, the more Bailey forgot to limp.

When we arrived, the girls had just gotten their ice cream, so there was no line. Bailey and I ordered and joined them.

"Mmmmm! This is deeeelish!" Nicola said, without getting any arguments.

"Hey Bailey, where did your family go on vacation last year?" Jenny asked.

"Nowhere. We didn't have enough money because of the drought."

"But you said you won your trophy while on vacation last year?" Jenny said.

What does Jenny know, I wondered.

"Oh, I thought you meant in addition to that vacation," Bailey said quickly.

"Where did you go on that vacation?" Jenny asked, smiling.

I was sure Jenny knew something, but what? And how did she find out?

"We went to Lake Geneva."

"Ooo, I've been there!" Becca said. "It's so pretty. My Grandpa took us out on his boat on that lake."

"We went to a . . ."

The conversations continued as everyone started sharing favorite vacations and lakes. Maybe Jenny noticed that Bailey wasn't limping any more when we got to the ice cream parlor. But, why had she asked Bailey earlier about the biggest lie she'd ever told?

Too many questions and not enough answers. I was getting more and more worried about Bailey. Not only was she lying, but her lies were getting bigger and more frequent. When would it all stop?

CHAPTER NINE

Spill the Beans

"Wow, girls! The float looks great!" my dad said. "I'm so proud of you."

"You helped a lot, too, Dad!" I added.

We had created a huge paper maché globe with strings of different-sized, colored handprints connected all around it. My dad suspended it between two posts so it would rotate during the parade. The entire bed of the truck was covered with tissue paper flowers with "Precious Girls Club" spelled out on each side. There was room for all of us to sit along the edge so we could toss out candy to little kids.

"Does everyone know where to meet for the start of the parade?" Dad asked.

We all nodded that we did.

"Today our job is cleanup," he said to a choir of moans and groans.

"Come on now! If we work together, it will go fast and I'll buy lunch at the Shine Burger Bar afterward!" he promised.

That got everyone moving.

Just when I thought Bailey's lying streak had finally ended, she proved me wrong.

"Is anybody going to the state fair next month?" she asked.

"I am!" came the answers from most girls.

"My grandma always enters a quilt in the contest," Lidia said.

"I remember the awards she showed us when we were at your house," Avery said.

"Who else has won an award at the state fair?" Becca asked.

"My family usually enters several categories," Bailey said.

"How cool! What category do you enter, Bailey?"

"I . . . umm . . . I won a blue ribbon for an apple pie one year," she lied again.

I couldn't believe my ears! What was she doing?

I didn't say anything, but I was getting tired of it. I waited until everyone went to wash their hands and I stayed behind with Bailey.

She looked up from the sink and saw me. "Don't say anything, okay?"

"Why do you keep lying?"

"I don't know what you mean," she said, heading for the door.

I decided to stand in front of it. "Bailey, I know you lied about the trophy and I know you lied about the pie. You have lied about all sorts of things lately!"

"Katie, it feels so good to have everybody think I did something special! I never get to feel that way."

"But Bailey, that's not true."

"I know!"

"Do you? It sounds a little like you've convinced yourself to believe them."

"Maybe I'm trying to."

"What do you mean?" I asked.

A tear slipped down Bailey's cheek and she turned away and got quiet.

"Bailey, talk to me, please!"

"It doesn't feel good to lie. It did at first, but then it made me feel twice as bad as when I hadn't pretended I had won anything at all. I knew I was a fake and a phony. Plus I'm always scared of getting caught and found out."

"Then why do you keep doing it?"

"I don't know. It just keeps getting worse. Now I don't know what to do."

She finally turned around to face me. She was crying and I reached out to give her a big hug.

"It doesn't matter, Bailey."

"Yes, it does," she sniffed.

"Remember when my dad told us that lie, then he told the truth and apologized?"

"Yes, but that was no big deal."

"Exactly, because he came clean. It might have been a bigger deal if we'd found out and he hadn't told us. We may have felt betrayed."

I handed Bailey some tissues as she tried to clean up her face and stop crying.

"Come clean and tell everyone that you lied and why. Isn't that better than Jenny McBride finding out the truth and telling everyone for you?"

"Does she know?" Bailey asked, worried.

"I'm not sure. She might be guessing. But she'll make a big deal about it, and you'll wind up looking ten times worse."

"I don't know if I can do it."

"Sure you can. We're your friends."

"But I've lied so many times lately."

"That's a good reason to get it over with," I told her. "It took a lot for me to be honest with you right now, you know."

Bailey looked up and smiled at me.

"I'm glad you were."

"Me too."

"Let me find the right time to tell everyone, okay?"

"Of course," I said as we started walking back to join the others. "Just don't wait too long."

"I won't."

CHAPTER TEN

And the Winner Is . . .

The minute I got home, dinner was waiting. I reached over to pet Patches, gobbled down my meal, and asked to be excused.

"You might consider helping your mother with dishes," Dad said.

"I will, but can I do something in my room first?"

"Okay," Dad said.

I rushed up the stairs and found Faith practicing for her big contest. I tried to get her attention, but she was too busy to talk to me. Disappointed, I plopped on my bed.

"What's wrong, Munchkin?"

I looked up startled by her voice.

"I wanted to talk with you, but I thought you were too busy . . ."

"For you? Never," she smiled.

"But I tried to get your attention, and you were dancing and . . . "

"I'm never too busy for you," Faith repeated.

"What about your contest?"

"What about it?"

"It's important to you," I said.

"Isn't it important to you?"

"I guess so. I hope you win, Faith. You're the best! There's nobody better than you. But some things are more important than contests, aren't they?"

"Oh, sweetie, yes! In fact, there really isn't a contest at all."

I was really confused. "I don't get it."

Faith laughed. "I was trying to prove a point to you."

"What point is that?"

"That some things are more important than contests and who's best."

"Ohhhh," I said.

"I think you forget that sometimes."

I nodded.

"You're not alone. If you read the Bible, you'll find that people were competitive back then too."

"They were come pet a what?"

"They were competitive. They wanted to know who was the best or the greatest."

"Who did God think was the best?"

"He didn't worry about that. He just wanted everyone to treat one another with love. When someone wanted to know who was the best or the greatest, God said we should pay more attention to being humble and serving others."

"Really? What does that mean, Faith?"

"God doesn't want us to be so full of ourselves that we think one person is greater than another. He wants us to help and serve each other. If everyone did that, we'd all be treated special."

"You're right!"

I told Faith all about Bailey's confession and agreement to tell the others.

"I'm so glad. I'm also happy you were there to encourage her to do the right thing."

• • •

That night as I went to bed, I prayed and asked God to help me to be more humble. I also asked Him to show me ways to be a better servant to others. Then I thanked Him for my family and friends.

CHAPTER ELEVEN

Fireworks!

"Okay girls, climb aboard!" Dad said as he and Anna climbed into the truck that would pull our float in the parade.

Not too far from us, we heard the music of the marching band at the start of the parade. The streets were filled with families, anxious to see this year's parade.

It was my first time in a parade. I was glad I was with my best friends. We brought bags of candy and little treats to toss to the kids along the way.

Our float inched its way to a place behind a group of men riding around in little cars. A dancing troupe followed behind. I couldn't believe how well they danced while moving along the streets of Shine.

"Katie! Hey, Katie!" I heard.

I turned my head and saw my mom, Aunt Ella,

Patches, and Moses sitting in front of the library. I waved and they waved and barked back. When the girls saw them, they bombarded them with candy and treats. Little kids dashed forward, scrambling to pick up every piece.

Kathleen called out to Bailey on the next block, "How's your ankle?"

Bailey gave her a "so-so" sign.

After the parade, I grabbed a burger with Bailey and headed for an empty table somewhere in the shade. I immediately asked, "When are you telling the others?"

"I don't know. Don't ruin today, okay?"

"But Jenny has a plan you won't like."

"Spill," Bailey said.

"I heard her talking to kids about your great success. She said they should make sure to get you as their partner in all the races later, because then they'd win."

"Oh no!"

"Bailey, you've got to tell them."

"But I'm not ready."

"I'll be right with you. Let's call everyone over and get it over with."

Bailey looked scared.

"Stay here. I'll flag everyone down. Just get it

over with. You'll feel better."

Once everyone was sitting together, Lidia asked, "So what's up?"

"This is a bad idea, Katie. People are everywhere," Bailey hissed.

She was right. Huge groups of people had arrived. The carnival rides were underway. Little kids were running around everywhere. I just looked at her, pleading.

"I'm the one who has something to say," Bailey finally blurted out.

Everyone waited patiently as Bailey summoned the courage to spit it out.

"Come on, Bailey! I'd like to get a snow cone before they're gone,"

"Okay, okay!" she said. "I lied."

That got everyone's attention.

"What do you mean?"

"I've never won anything, and I felt awful because all of you had many special things you've done. I had nothing, so I made it up. It's my sister's

73

trophy and my mom's blue ribbon pie. I don't have any awards at all."

Bailey looked sad. The other girls looked both sad and surprised too.

"Bailey, what do you mean *'nothing'*?" Nicola asked. "You're very talented!"

Bailey smiled a little.

"You're much better than I am when it comes to making crafts," Avery said.

"We loved you before we thought you won that award. Why would we stop now?" Kirina asked. "Thanks for being honest."

I looked at Jenny who chose to remain silent. I took a breath of relief.

"Okay, you guys," I said. "Bailey needs our help today. It's full of games and contests, so everyone wants to be her partner. Let's save her from being embarrassed by each signing up to do an activity with her all day."

Everyone agreed! I could tell Jenny's plans were ruined, but even she agreed to help out as we all chose a fun activity to do with Bailey throughout the day.

"I really appreciate your forgiveness," Bailey added before we left to play games. "And I'm so thankful for your friendship, Katie. I'm glad I finally told the truth."

"Me too."

The rest of the day was a ton of fun. We tossed water balloons and eggs. We made our way through a crazy hay bale maze and joined in a three-legged race, a wheelbarrow race, and a water relay.

The day was topped off with a display of fireworks. As we sat on the lawn, Mayor McGuire led us in the Pledge of Allegiance and we sang "America the Beautiful".

"I have a special announcement to make before our skies light up with color," he said. "I'm very proud to announce that a group of girls in our community has been chosen as one of ten groups from all around the country as *Today's Students for a Better Tomorrow!* Would the Precious Girls Club please come forward?"

We couldn't believe what we were hearing. We jumped up and down as everyone applauded.

"Girls, my congratulations. We're very proud of you. I'll let each of you read the letter from the President later, but I do want to read just one portion of it:

> *. . . one of the significant reasons that your group was chosen is due to the wonderful essays that were submitted. It was very clear*

that your group was committed to helping, supporting, and celebrating the gifts that God gave each one of you. In turn, you have chosen to use those gifts to help others and provide positive services within your community . . .

"What a wonderful gift to our community and a terrific example to those around you. On behalf of our little town, I want to thank each of you."

The crowd applauded and the sky lit up with an explosion of color! There were several crackles and a big BOOM!

We watched the display splash through the sky. Afterward, my dad gathered us together and gave us a small gift.

"What is it, Dad?" I asked.

"It's a key charm. I know that you girls enjoy playing *Truth or Dare.* So I decided to give you the key to truth to remind you how important it is to be honest."

He didn't know just how much his gift meant to all of us that night.

"Look how nice it looks on our charm bracelets!" Lidia said, showing it off.

I grabbed Bailey and gave her something else. It was a musical snow globe with a beautiful angel inside of it.

"Look how pretty!" Bailey said. "Thank you so much! What's her name?"

"Alecia. It means *truthful one*," I smiled.

That night, Anna and I gathered with Mom and Dad to say goodnight. We were both sleepy, but Mom had a poem that she had written. She read it to us.

As fireworks splash throughout the sky
I look to the heavens, and wonder why
I was so blessed with girls like you
Who light up my life and love me back too.
You're growing up fast with honesty and grace,
I am so proud to look upon your face.
Hold to your values, always believe,
Let truth be the goal you want to achieve.
Always remember you are loved and held dear,
From way high above—and by those so near.

A Charmed
Life Is Precious

Make a beautiful bracelet that tells your story and shows how precious you truly are.

Honesty Charm

We earned our Honesty charm in this book! It's always best to be honest! Honesty is the key!

Friendship Charm

Respect Charm

Kind Charm

Up next for the Precious Girls Club: Book #6

Lost and Found

The winds howled around our tents as the thunder rolled in. Each drop of rain sounded like it would punch right through the canvas of our tents. Lightning flashed, causing the inside to brighten up before going dark again.

In the morning, the sun was shining, everything smelled wonderful, and our tents were dry.

"This week went by too fast," Avery moaned.

"Not for Jenny," I said.

"Speaking of which, where is she?" Mom asked.

"Still sleeping," Becca answered.

"I'll wake her!" Kirina offered.

"What kind of mood is she in today?" Nicola asked when Kirina returned.

"She wasn't there," Kirina said, running back from her tent, "Jenny's backpack and sleeping bag are gone too! I think she ran away!"

"Do you think she was out in that terrible storm all night?" Lidia asked.

"No way. Jenny hates getting wet," Nicola answered.

"But what if she left before the storm began?"

The question hung in the air. No one wanted to answer it. Each group silently took off, hoping to find Jenny soon.

Read more in Lost and Found
in stores Winter 2009